Mary and the Twelve Months

Retold by Sean Taylor
Illustrated by Bee Willey

Once, a woodcutter lived in the forest with his wife and his daughter, Mary. But Mary's mother died, so her father looked after Mary alone. He showed her all the love he could and they were happy in their small house.

But Mary's father married a new wife, and she had a daughter. They hated Mary. They made her sweep and scrub and wash and do all the things they didn't want to do.

One day, Mary's father said to his wife, "Today, I'll be working deep in the forest. I'll be back late. Will you take good care of Mary?"

"Of course," said the stepmother.

But as soon as Mary's father had left, she and her daughter were thinking up a way to get rid of Mary.

The stepmother said, "Mary, I want to make a strawberry pie. Go and find some strawberries."

It was January. Mary didn't think she would find any strawberries. But she took a basket and set off into the shadows of the forest.

The path twisted through the trees. Mary looked everywhere, but she found no strawberries.

Snow began to fall, and it became so dark she didn't know which way to go home. She was cold and lost. But then she saw something – a fire. "At least I'll be able to warm myself," she thought.

Sitting around the fire were twelve small men with beards, boots and caps. One of them jumped up and said, "Welcome, Mary! Come and warm yourself."

"How do you know my name?" Mary asked.

"We know names," said the man. "I'm January."

"My brothers and I are the twelve months of the year. Now, is there some way we can help you?"

"Well," Mary told him, "my stepmother sent me to find strawberries, but I haven't found any."

January smiled. "This is a job for July!"

So July took Mary's basket and was back in no time. The basket was full of ripe, red strawberries. Then January showed Mary the way home.

Mary's stepmother was amazed. But she didn't ask any questions.

Some days later, Mary's father said to his wife, "I have to go to the town. I'll be back late. Will you take good care of Mary?"

"Of course," she said.

But as soon as he left, she and her daughter were thinking up a way to get rid of Mary.

The stepmother said, "Mary, I want to make a blackberry pie. Go and find some blackberries."

Mary took the basket. This time, she knew where to go. She walked along the path. And, sure enough, she saw the fire.

Up jumped January. "Welcome, Mary! Come and warm yourself. Now, is there some way we can help you?"

"Well," Mary told him, "my stepmother sent me to find blackberries, but I haven't found any."

January smiled. "This is a job for September!"

So September took Mary's basket and was back in no time. The basket was full of juicy blackberries. Then September showed Mary the way home.

Mary's stepmother was amazed. This time she couldn't keep quiet.

"It's winter!" she said. "Where did you get blackberries?"

Mary told her stepmother about the fire and the twelve brothers. Her stepmother shouted, "Foolish girl! You asked for strawberries and blackberries? You could have asked for diamonds and pearls! Quickly, daughter! We'll go ourselves!"

So they made Mary show them the way to the fire.

January jumped up. “Welcome! Come and warm yourselves,” he said. “Now, is there some way we can help you?”

“We want diamonds and pearls!” said Mary’s stepmother.

January smiled. “This is a job for March!”

March stood up, and a great whistling, whirling March wind blew through the trees. It tugged at the stepmother and the stepsister, and lifted them off the ground. It swept them higher and higher, up into the diamonds and pearls of the night sky.

And they were never heard of again.

Mary's father came home. From that day on, he looked after her alone. He showed Mary all the love he could and they were happy in their small house.